# DUCK
# BOY

# Christobel Mattingley

# DUCK BOY

## Illustrated by Patricia Mullins

A Margaret K. McElderry Book
ATHENEUM 1986 NEW YORK

To Barb, Jim, Peter and Ruth,
and Patricia too.

**Library of Congress Cataloging-in-Publication Data**

Mattingley, Christobel.
   Duck boy.
   "A Margaret K. McElderry book."
   Summary: Adam's vacation on a farm doesn't go well until he befriends
two ducks who need his protection.
   1. Children's stories [1. Ducks–Fiction.
2. Farm life–Fiction]   I. Mullins, Patricia ill.
II. Title.
PZ7.M43543Du   1986      [E]        85-7521
ISBN 0-689-50361-X

Text copyright © 1983 by Christobel Mattingley
Illustrations copyright © 1983 by Angus & Robertson Publishers
First published by Angus & Robertson Publishers, Sydney, Australia, 1983

Printed and bound in the U.S.A.
First American edition

# CONTENTS

# 1 LEFT OUT

It was almost dark when they arrived at the farm. All that Adam could see was the deep rippled river running beside the house and the tall bush crowding in on the paddocks around. It was the first time Adam had been away for a holiday without his parents and it seemed rather lonely, though of course Steve and Kate were with him.

"Time to explore in the morning," Mrs Perry said, as she showed them where they were to sleep.

Steve and Kate grabbed the top bunks. "And don't you go waking us too early," they said to Adam.

But it was kookaburras that woke them soon after daybreak. Steve swung his long legs down so that his toes were almost tickling Adam's nose. "Let's get going," he said.

At the back of the shed behind the truck and the old tractor Steve found a canoe. He scouted around among the heaps of tires and spares, tools and crates until he unearthed the paddle. He examined everything carefully. "Looks OK to me, but I suppose I'd better ask before I use them." He picked up the paddle and went through the motions with it.

"Can I have a turn?" Adam asked. Steve passed over the paddle and as Adam balanced it in his hands he looked at the river dancing gold in the sun and wondered how it would feel to be floating on the quiet water.

Kate had noticed a saddle hanging on the wall and was staring into the paddocks. "Look! There's a horse!" She set off at a run. Adam followed. By the time he caught up with her, she had slowed to a walk and was within a few meters of the horse. But as he panted up, the horse wheeled and galloped away.

2

Kate turned on him. "Why did you have to scare it?"

Adam looked at the dappled rump and wished that he was sitting on it as it rocked across the green paddock towards the trees. "I wonder what his name is? Dandelion, do you think? Or Drummer?"

Kate did not answer. They walked in silence back to the house.

At breakfast Steve asked Mrs Perry about the canoe.

"Yes, it's seaworthy all right, and you can use it provided you always wear the life jacket. But you must be very careful and keep a good lookout. The river isn't as peaceful as it seems. Water-skiers often use this stretch and the boats come round the curve at quite a speed."

"What about the horse?" Kate was very keen on riding.

Mrs Perry laughed. "Daisy? You can ride her if you can catch her. She's quite safe. But she's used to her freedom. Be sure you wear your hard hat."

After breakfast Steve said, "Give us a hand, Adam, to carry the canoe down to the water." Adam jumped up and was at the shed before Steve. He dusted the canoe down carefully with an old rag and put in the paddle. Steve arrived carrying the life jacket Mrs Perry had given him.

"This is the best way," Steve said, taking the lead and heading down the bank at a point beyond the vegetable patch where it sloped more gently. They slid the canoe into the water. Steve climbed in and started to push off.

"Can't I come too?" Adam asked.

"It's only a one-man," Steve said. "And besides, there's only one life jacket."

Steve dipped the paddle and as he lifted it, Adam watched the water droplets running down the blade. Like tears. He waited on the bank, watching every movement of the paddle and the growing wake of water as the canoe drew further and further away. He waited, and it seemed as if the canoe would never come back. At last Steve turned and the canoe came skimming. Skimming towards Adam, still waiting on the bank.

"It's my turn now," Adam called. But his voice was drowned by the buzz of a speedboat coming round the curve like an angry red bee, with a water-skier weaving behind like a crazy black wasp. The canoe

4

wallowed in their wash, which was still slapping at the banks after the boat and skier had disappeared beyond the next curve. It continued to rock even after Steve had pulled in to the bank.

"My turn now," Adam repeated.

But Steve shook his head. "Sorry, mate. You can't swim well enough, and that crew has to come back some time. It's not safe."

Adam scowled at the fading ripples of the powerboat's wake and did not look as Steve pushed out into the stream again. He yanked at a tussock and as the grass came away in his hand he remembered the horse. Daisy. He'd been nearly right about her name. He'd go and see Daisy.

The saddle was missing from its peg, so Kate must have gone down the paddock already. He wondered if she had managed to catch Daisy yet. If she was as difficult as Mrs Perry said, it might be useful to have some tidbits.

He went back to the house. "May I have an apple, please?" he asked Mrs Perry, who was making bread.

"Help yourself, love," she said, pointing with her elbow to a bowl on the dresser.

5

"Grannies. Grown on the place," she added proudly. "Just watch out as you eat them though. You might find the occasional grub. Didn't get the trees sprayed in time last season."

Adam pocketed three apples. He didn't think Daisy would mind a grub or two. He was almost out the door when Mrs Perry called him back. "I haven't taken the scraps up to the chooks," she said. "I thought you might like to do it. The bucket's in the porch."

Adam looked sourly at the bucket. Who cared about hens when there was a horse? But Mrs Perry seemed to think she was giving him a treat, so he didn't like to refuse. He hurried up the track to the yard where thirty or more fowls were scratching in the dust. They saw him coming and flocked around the gate, jostling and impatient like a crowd at the entrance to a football ground.

As Adam slung the bucket and the scraps showered across the yard the chickens scattered in a squawking skelter. The rooster, who had been keeping to himself, bore down and swept aside a scrum of hens. When the flurry of gobbling and quarrelling had passed, a few hens came up to Adam. They cocked their heads to look inquisitively at his hands and one pecked at his toe where a piece of potato peel had dropped on his thong. Adam thumped the bucket to show that it was empty and they all ran off to the other end of the yard.

"Suits me if you don't want to stay and be friendly," he said. "I'd sooner be with the horse anyway." He thudded the gate shut and jabbed the latch into its socket, dropped the bucket in the porch and set off at a gallop in search of Daisy.

Kate had already found her, but Adam could see from a distance that she had not been able to get the bridle on, let alone the saddle. He walked up very slowly, whistling softly and taking care not to startle Daisy. When he saw that she was watching him he stopped and pulled an apple from his pocket. He'd only taken two bites when Daisy started to move towards him. He held out the apple to her and in a moment he felt her soft moist breath on his flat stretched fingers and saw her strong yellow teeth biting into the apple. "That's a good girl, Daisy," he said, stroking her forehead. "I didn't think you'd be fussy about a grub."

Kate was already slipping on the bridle. "Simple," she said. "I'll bring an apple myself tomorrow."

"I've brought one for you too," Adam said.

"Just hold her a moment, will you?" Kate said, and tossed the blanket over. "Now help me with this strap." The saddle creaked as she pulled on the girth. Adam breathed in the smell of horse and leather eagerly. Kate adjusted the stirrups, swung herself up into the saddle, and Daisy was off.

Adam watched as she drummed across

the grass, throwing up little tufts and clods as she went. Round the paddock she went and round again. Adam was not quite sure whether it was Kate or Daisy choosing the course. At last they cantered back to where he was standing.

"What are you waiting for?" Kate wanted to know.

"My turn, of course," Adam said.

"But you can't ride," Kate said. "And you'll have to wait for a couple of days at least until she quietens down before you can try. She could throw you or wipe you off on a tree in the mood she's in now, and you haven't even got a riding cap."

"What about yours?" Adam said.

"It wouldn't fit you," Kate said, and wheeled away.

Adam began walking back even more slowly than he had come. Suddenly he heard hooves behind. He looked round. Perhaps Kate would give him a ride after all. But all she said was, "You forgot to give me my apple."

Adam handed up the apple. But he did not warn her about the grub.

# 2 DISCOVERY

Adam mooched back in the direction of the house. By the shed a cat was lying in the sun. "Hullo, pussy," he said, going towards it. But before he could lean down to stroke it, the cat had jumped away. It leaped on to some hay bales beside the shed and Adam scrambled after it. The bales were stacked like giant steps, but by the time he had climbed to the top the cat was already halfway along the roof ridge. Adam decided not to follow.

From the stack he could see down to the river and right across the paddocks. He sat and watched Steve paddling upstream and

11

Kate and Daisy canter the length of the most distant paddock. But it wasn't much fun just watching, and after a while the hay began to prick his bottom and scratch his legs.

He looked around for the cat. It was nowhere to be seen. But up on the fence was the rooster, a handsome bird, his feathers glittering in the sun like a bunch of Christmas baubles. Adam decided he was worth a closer look.

He slithered down from the haystack and stalked towards the fowl yard. "Let's see your tail," Adam coaxed. "I promise I won't pull out any feathers." But the wily rooster kept his distance and Adam became impatient. "There you are, chooks," he called and threw the apple core he had intended for the rooster to the fowls. There was a scurry and a squabble around him, but when nothing remained of the apple core Adam was ignored once more. So he turned his back on the fowls.

What to do next? And who to talk to? There was only Mrs Perry. The dough kneading had looked rather fun. He wouldn't mind having a go at that.

Too late. There was a hot smell of bread

coming from the kitchen and Mrs Perry was at the sink washing up.

"Can I help?" Adam asked.

Mrs Perry handed him a tea towel.

"I mean with the dough," Adam said.

"Thanks, Adam, but it's all done. You're just in time to help eat it though."

While Adam was wiping the big mixing bowl she went to the oven and pulled out a tray of shiny rolls, with curly brown tops speckled with sesame seeds.

"What are they?" Adam wanted to know.

"Snails."

"Did you really make them?" Adam asked. "They look like the fancy rolls in the continental shop at home." With his finger he traced the curving crust in the air.

"Yes." Mrs Perry smiled at him. "Mr Perry was as partial as a duck to his snails. But I haven't made them since he passed on. Stan always preferred his plain loaf of bread. All the same, my hand hasn't lost its touch," she said proudly. "Try one." She pushed the tray towards him. "Don't burn your mouth. Have a glass of milk while you're waiting for it to cool." She fetched milk and butter from the refrigerator.

"Where's Stan now?" Adam asked.

"He's away in the city," Mrs Perry replied.

"Will he be home soon?"

Mrs Perry shook her head and looked rather sad. "No, he lives there now. That's why things are all behind round the place. He married a city girl — long painted fingernails and strappy high heels — you know the sort. She doesn't like the farm. They're saving up to buy their own house in town. Oh, Stan does come down occasionally for a weekend and do some jobs for me, but it's not the same."

Adam felt sorry for Mrs Perry. "Can I do some jobs for you?" he asked.

"Bless you." Mrs Perry laid an arm around Adam's shoulders. "You're here to have a lovely holiday. It's a great place for kids. Stan always loved it. That's his canoe. And Daisy is his. Seeing it doesn't look as if I'm going to have any grandchildren for a while, I thought it was time somebody's children had the use of the place. Now you run along and enjoy yourself and don't fuss your head about an old woman's troubles. Take some more rolls with you, and you needn't worry about coming back until you're hungry again. There are lots of places to explore. You'll probably want to stay out all day.''

Adam was not so sure, but he didn't like to say so. He stuffed his pockets with rolls and apples. ''See you,'' he called, as the door banged behind him.

He wandered upstream along the bank, jabbing a stick into horse droppings, switching at the long heads of paspalum grass, throwing stones in the wake of water-skiers. Once a skier fell off at the curve and Adam cheered. Steve waved from over the other side of the river and Adam wished they could change places. The far bank was formed by low red sandstone cliffs and Adam could see a fold in the rocks that looked like a cave. That would be the place to explore. He wished he could swim better so that Steve would let him use the canoe. But the banks on this side sloped steeply and the water ran fast and deep. He had seen nowhere he could practise and prove himself to Steve.

Then suddenly he discovered the perfect place.

A little creek running down from the bushy hillside to join the river had formed a quiet backwater, and a huge old willow tree screened it from the main stream. Adam surveyed it in excitement. It was like his own private swimming pool. And the canopy of willow was like a ready-made cubby hole. He lifted aside some branches to investigate.

There was a hissing and a snapping. Adam jumped, dropped the branches and stepped back hastily. The hissing grew louder as a flash of white burst out through the greenery and a slash of red streaked towards his ankles. Adam retreated further, then stopped. He almost began to laugh when he saw that it was only a duck. He had always thought of ducks as rather friendly creatures. But this one was not. It kept on advancing towards him, neck outstretched, wings flapping. Adam continued to retreat until he evidently reached neutral ground and the duck stopped. Then they stood and stared at each other, until Adam re-membered the rolls in his pockets and threw some pieces as a sign of truce.

But the duck did not allow itself to be won over so easily. It held its position, still staring fiercely at him with its bean-black eyes, and Adam did not feel like making

16

any move that might annoy it. That broad
bill with its ugly red clump of blisters
looked a nasty weapon. Finally the duck
made a move towards the creek, and
although on land it had seemed almost
grotesque, Adam had to admire it when it
took to the water. If only he could swim like
that.

He looked at the creek and wondered if
he dared to take the plunge. It might be over
his depth, there might be snags. There
might be other things in it besides the duck
rippling across the surface. And even if
there weren't he felt sure the duck would
make him most unwelcome. He sat on a log
and crunched up what was left of the roll

while he watched the duck's stately progress across the pool. By the time he had licked the last sesame seeds off his fingers, the duck had decided to go about its own business and was grazing on the far side.

Adam saw his chance to spy into the territory that the duck had been defending, and crept round behind the willow tree. After the bright light glinting on the water, it was hard to see in the green gloom under the tree. For a moment when Adam glimpsed a ghostly white glimmer and heard a low plaintive sound, he was almost scared. Then he began to grin. For the second time that day he'd been surprised by a duck.

But this duck made no hostile attack. It stayed where it was, crouching over the ground. Adam wondered if it was hurt and was walking over to have a closer look when there was a hissing and a snapping behind him. Without looking round he knew that his ankles were in danger. He grabbed a bough above him and swung his legs clear.

The angry duck took up guard beside the other. Adam did not care to risk trying an escape, so he made himself as comfortable as possible in the tree. The big duck seemed

18

very friendly towards the sitting duck, almost seemed to be looking after it, and Adam decided that the smaller duck was probably sick.

The big duck was in no hurry to go back to the water, so Adam took out his last apple to eat while he waited. He had munched almost to the core when he came across one of the curling white grubs Mrs Perry had warned of. He shook it off and it fell just in front of the sitting duck, which snapped it up. Adam remembered the bread snail still in his other pocket.

He took aim carefully and dropped a piece in front of each duck at the same time, then another two pieces, and two more. Then he slithered along the bough and dropped gently to the ground a respectful distance from the ducks. Before the big duck could take the offensive, Adam threw more bread and the ducks accepted it graciously.

"I won't hurt you," Adam told them. "And if you'll let me," he said to the big duck, "I'll help you look after your sick friend. I'll bring you food," he promised, "and perhaps you'll let me swim in your pool?"

# 3 RATS!

When Adam got back to the house, Steve and Kate were already there.

"Would you like to help me carry the canoe up?" Steve asked.

"Will you help me groom Daisy?" Kate asked.

Adam shook his head. "Sorry. I want to do a few jobs for Mrs Perry. I'm going to feed the chooks and collect the eggs."

After the ducks, the fowls seemed quite undignified, milling about and mobbing him when he appeared with the feed tin. Adam quickly decided that the ducks were his favorites and pocketed a large handful of the chicken feed for them.

When he brought the eggs in, Mrs Perry said, "What a help you are, Adam. Did you have a good day?"

Adam nodded. "I found a sort of a pool."

Mrs Perry was pleased. "You found the creek," she exclaimed. "Not everyone does. It was always one of Stan's special places. He learned to swim there. It's so much safer for beginners than the river. There's an old inner tube in the shed you can take down there if you like, for a raft."

It was Adam's turn to be pleased. "But don't tell the others about it, will you?" he was saying just as they came back.

"What's the secret? What aren't we supposed to hear about?" they wanted to know.

Adam was determined to surprise them by teaching himself to swim really well and claiming his right to the canoe. He had to keep his pool private at all costs, so he tried to change the subject.

"I met a duck today. It was rather fierce."

Steve laughed. "Just as well you weren't in the canoe. If a dangerous duck had charged, you might have capsized."

Kate laughed too. "And if it had charged

the horse, you might have been thrown.''

They went off laughing together to wash their hands, and Adam said to Mrs Perry, ''I did see a duck today and it was fierce. I saw two ducks, but the other one was sort of sad and sick looking. Its chest was bare and moulty.''

''That must be Lucy and The General,'' Mrs Perry said, and Adam could tell she was pleased again. ''Lucy must be broody. Poor dears, they try so hard, but they never succeed in raising a family. Something always happens.''

''What happens?'' Adam wanted to know.

''Well, Lucy is a very good mother and always makes a nice soft nest. And The General is very fierce, as you say, and does his best to protect it. But even The General is no match for rats and goannas and foxes.''

''Goannas? What are they?''

''A sort of giant lizard as long as you are tall. They love eggs and there's a really big fellow comes down from the hillside every so often for a feed.''

''Couldn't Stan catch him?''

''He didn't try,'' Mrs Perry said.

22

"Goannas have a right to live and after all, they were here in the bush long before the farms came. But I must say I don't have so much sympathy for the rats and foxes. Cunning brutes," she added with a burst of feeling.

"How long will Lucy be broody? Will the ducklings hatch out before I have to go?"

Steve and Kate came back looking for dinner and overheard Adam's last questions.

"A fierce duck and a broody duck. You're in for an exciting holiday," Steve said.

"Playing nursemaid to a duck." Kate laughed.

Adam said nothing and neither did Mrs Perry. But Adam noticed that she slipped the crispiest baked potato on to his plate and dabbed an extra lump of butter on his beans. And she gave him the extra piece of lemon meringue tart that was left over. Adam decided that she felt the same way about Steve and Kate and him as he felt about the fowls and the ducks.

In the morning after he had fed the fowls, Adam brought in a broken eggshell to show Mrs Perry. "I found it quite a long way outside the yard," he said. "How did it get there?"

Mrs Perry looked at the shell, which had only the merest trace of yolk still clinging to it. "Rats," she said with disgust. "They can carry an egg a surprisingly long way."

"Can't you do something about them? Poison them or trap them?"

"They get wary of traps. Mr Perry used to shoot them. He was a great shot. And Stan had a dog that was a terrific ratter. I tried laying poison down, but the trouble is I like to let the chooks out to forage, and they must have picked up some of the baits, because a couple of them died. So I gave up the poisoning."

"What about the cat? Doesn't she catch them?"

"Poor old Smutty. There are too many for her. We always used to have a whole family of cats about the place. But Tom was bitten by a brown snake last autumn and poor Jerry got caught in the neighbor's fox trap in the winter. So there were no kittens this spring, and Smutty is fighting a losing battle with the rats, I'm afraid."

"Did you let the chooks out yesterday?"

"No," said Mrs Perry. "I forgot. I was

enjoying the extra cooking so much, I quite forgot the chooks.''

Adam said, "I'll look after them for you. I'll feed them and collect the eggs, and let them out and shut them in. And I'll lay rat baits in the afternoon when the chooks are back in their yard and I'll pick them up in the mornings before I let the chooks out.''

Mrs Perry looked pleased. "If we had a real blitz on the rats for a month, that would make a difference.'' Then she sounded doubtful. "But I don't know whether I should be letting you touch poison.''

Adam drew himself up. "I'm not a baby," he said. "I won't do anything silly. And I promise I'll wash my hands afterwards every single time.''

Mrs Perry smiled at him. "Of course you're not a baby. I've needed a helper around the place for a long time, and now I've got one. Come along, we'll get the poisoned wheat fixed straight away, ready for tonight, and I have to show you your inner tube too. It'll need pumping up.''

In the shed Mrs Perry pointed to the bin on a high shelf where the poisoned wheat was kept. "The trouble is, the rats have no

25

manners and they scatter it everywhere and the chooks scratch it up."

"Leave it to me," said Adam. "I'll fix it."

He found ten large sheets of metal and on to each one he nailed a shallow tin. He showed Mrs Perry what he had done. "They can't knock any of these tins over, and anything they scatter can be collected off the sheet."

Mrs Perry nodded her approval. "Like cups and saucers. That's clever," she said. "You've got to be clever to beat the rats." She helped Adam connect the pump to the inner tube and together they watched the flabby black ring grow full and hard.

"I'll make a sledge for it," Adam said. "It would be fun to roll it but I don't want it to get a puncture." He found an old wooden door and tied a rope to the handle. Mrs Perry stowed a bag of lunch for him and a bag of bread for the ducks in the middle of the tube, and Adam set off. He was glad that Steve was already down on the river and that Kate was well away on Daisy, so that they didn't see him and couldn't make fun of him or spoil his secret.

# 4 CAMPAIGN

It was heavy work dragging the sledge over the bumpy ground and Adam stopped several times for a rest. Just before he got within sight of the pool he paused to consider his tactics. He did not want to alarm The General by suddenly appearing with such a juggernaut. So he left the sledge and began to reconnoiter, crawling up the slope on his stomach to overlook the pool.

The General was afloat out in the middle, but there was no sign of Lucy. Adam sat up so that The General could see him and called, "Hullo, General. How's the water today?"

The General turned and swam pur-
posefully to the near bank. He came out
of the water and began marching up
towards Adam. But today he didn't look so
fierce. Adam went on talking. "Mrs Perry
sent her compliments to you and her love to
your wife. She's pleased to hear Lucy's in
the family way again. And we're starting a
special campaign against the rats tonight. I
want to see your babies on the pool before I
go."

The General came within a few steps of
Adam but made no offensive move. He
looked at Adam, with his head slightly on
one side. He seemed to be considering. It
was as if he had decided that Adam was his
ally, because suddenly he squatted down as
if he were tired and tucked his head under
his wing.

"OK, old fellow," Adam said. "My turn
for sentry duty."

Adam sat beside the sleeping duck and
looked out over their joint territory. A light
breeze was tickling the surface of the water
and fluttering the curtain of leaves which
screened Lucy. Two sea-green dragon flies
were hovering near a clump of bulrushes,
and on a low tree branch on the far side a

kingfisher was poised, like a blade of blue. Some frogs were gossiping together in the shallows and over the center of the pool a troupe of swallows was performing its aerobatics. It was a peaceful scene. Adam felt sorry for Lucy, shut away from it all.

Then, without warning, an enemy had arrived. Adam caught sight of a movement in the bushes on the hill where the creek came down, and watched intently. A long grey form like a little crocodile slid out of the cover and started running at speed towards the willow tree.

"General!" Adam shouted, jumping to his feet. "It's the goanna! Quick! Head him off!"

He grabbed a stick and an old can which was lying nearby and ran between the goanna and the willow tree, beating his makeshift drum and whooping at the top of his voice.

The goanna veered away and headed up towards the bush again. Adam followed, yelling, banging, crashing through the undergrowth, snapping sticks, crunching the crisp dead leaves which littered the ground. At last he stopped, puffing and hot. The goanna had disappeared in the

29

distance up the hill.

"He won't come back again in a hurry," Adam announced to The General. "But just to make sure, we'll have to patrol regularly. And I'll make some ammunition dumps." He collected piles of stones and decided he'd bring some more old cans from the shed for extra drums.

He wondered if Lucy had been disturbed by all the noise. He wanted to go and talk with her, but he didn't like to do it without The General's permission. So he thought about how he might launch his tube and whether The General would approve of this new intruder.

The General himself solved everything by taking the lead when Adam started back to the sledge. The big drake inspected the door and the tube and felt no need to accept the bribe of bread Adam offered. He left it lying on the ground and turned towards the willow tree, looking back several times to see that Adam was following. He led him straight to Lucy, who greeted him with soft, almost soundless throaty pleasure. After she had taken some of the pieces of bread Adam threw down in front of her, The General ate a crust himself.

30

Adam was longing to see Lucy's eggs. How many were tucked away there in the feather bed under her breast? She moved gently from time to time, re-settling herself with great care, nudging the eggs closer together with her bill, murmuring softly as she did so. She seemed happy to stay all day without leaving the nest and Adam had almost given up hope of catching even a glimpse of the eggs, when suddenly she got up and walked away.

Adam stared down at the nest. One, two, three, four, five, six, seven, eight, nine, ten, eleven, twelve, thirteen eggs. Thirteen eggs, longer and larger than hens' eggs, smooth and heavy, the color of weathered bone. And inside each egg a baby duck was growing. Adam wondered how long it would be before they hatched. In his mind's eye he could see them already swimming on the pool behind their mother, like little spoonfuls of lemon meringue.

He was still egg-gazing when Lucy came back. "They're beautiful, Lucy. They're just beautiful. Thank you for showing me."

Lucy settled herself and Adam and The General went back to the sledge. Adam did not want to disturb Lucy by dragging the sledge down the slope, so he half carried, half rolled the tube down to the creek. It hit the water with the sound of a belly flop and started to move out towards the center. But The General was not worried. He swam beside it as escort.

Adam kicked off his thongs, pulled off his shirt and waded out into the water. The bottom was squelchy under his feet and he didn't like the feel of it. He threw himself forward and began to kick, reaching out towards the tube. He grabbed it but it bounced out of reach, and each time it was

almost within his grasp it slipped away again.

Kicking and puffing, Adam caught it at last. He pulled himself up, looked around and found that he had swum to the other side. He decided that the tube had too much air and that he didn't have enough. He let some out of the tube, and when he had completed the return swim he was not even out of breath. Back and forth he swam, with The General beside him all the way. Then he sat in the sun and ate an apple. And The General ate the core. Tomorrow he would swim the length of the pool. His legs were tired as he walked home, but he was very happy.

He collected the eggs and hustled the chickens back into their yard, so that he could get on with laying the poison baits. The sooner those rats were dealt with, the better. He placed each tray carefully and hoped the rats were feeling hungry.

The rats were very hungry. Not only did they sample the poisoned wheat, they also killed three chickens. Adam found the remains of the little mangled bodies next morning when he went to fill the water bowl in their special pen. He looked around and discovered a place where the rats had gnawed a hole in the boards at the back and another place where they had tunnelled under the wire netting.

He called Mrs Perry. Together they inspected the damage. Adam filled the hole under the fence with stones and nailed a piece of metal across the nesting box. "What about Lucy?" he asked anxiously.

"Rats are very partial to ducklings, as well as eggs," Mrs Perry said, "as Lucy knows."

"I think I'd better build her a pen," Adam said. "Is there some wire I can have?"

At the back of the shed Mrs Perry showed him some rolls of netting, with the grass growing through them. "Stan was going to fix the fences," she said.

Adam wrenched out a length of close-meshed netting and Mrs Perry found metal posts, staples, wire for binding, a spade and a mallet. "Too much to carry," Adam decided. So he went off to fetch the sledge.

He was relieved to find Lucy sitting snugly on her eggs. "We'll soon have you safe behind a proper fence," Adam told her. "Then your worries will be over," he told The General.

He trudged back a second time with the loaded sledge and started right in on the job. Adam measured out the enclosure, then he drove in the metal posts, one at each corner. The ground under the willow tree was damp and they all went in easily, except one which struck a root. He had to move that one a little so that it was slightly out of line. But it was a pretty good start. He and The General went for their first swim to celebrate, and did a length of the pool.

Adam was determined that the rats would not burrow under his fence. Watched by Lucy and The General he began to dig a trench. It was hard work. The soil was matted with roots and after he had been toiling for half an hour, there wasn't much to show for it. But the ducks found it very rewarding as the spade turned up various creatures. Adam pounced on the fattest worms and tossed them to Lucy, while The General foraged for himself.

Adam took time off for his second swim, then returned to slog away at his trench. He had hoped to make it thirty centimeters deep so that he could bury the base of the wire, but at the rate he was going it was not likely to be more than ten. Lucy stretched her legs for a little while and inspected the work at close quarters. She looked at Adam so trustingly that he postponed his next swim and put on another spurt.

He stuck a twig up in the trench at each point where he stopped for a swim and the day wore on — dig, swim, dig, swim, dig, lunch, dig, swim, dig, apple, dig, swim — until there were thirteen twigs. But the trench was not finished. Adam was very discouraged. The sun was getting low and he had to go back to feed the fowls. Tonight he'd just have to put up a makeshift fence after all.

He unrolled the wire and fixed it at the corners as best he could with string. Tomorrow he'd do better. He couldn't work out how to make a gate and he didn't know how The General would take being shut in like a silly chook, but it seemed the only thing to do. He threw the last of the scraps he'd brought for them down beside Lucy and while The General was eating his share, Adam tied up the ends of the wire netting. He dragged two heavy stones up from the river bank to make it as secure as he could. Then he stacked his tools under the sledge and waved goodbye.

# 5 TO THE RESCUE

There were grumbling clouds over the hillside and the wind was muttering up in the trees. Adam hurried, in case Mrs Perry should think he had forgotten and do the fowls herself. He had just brought in the eggs when the first rain began to fall in heavy drops. It sounded like a giant shaking a colander of peas over the roof. Adam was worried. "Do you think Lucy and The General will be all right?" he asked Mrs Perry.

She laughed and ladled him a big bowl full of tomato soup from a pot bubbling on the stove. "Home grown and home made," she told him proudly. "Not like that red sludge out of cans. And you know what they say about rain, don't you? Nice weather for ducks!"

But later on that night, when Adam snuggled warm and cosy in his bed, he could not get any comfort from the saying. It was as if the giant had run out of peas to shake on the roof and had popped the house in his washing machine. As the wind swirled and whirled round corners and the rain rushed and swished over the roof, it didn't sound like nice weather for anything.

Steve and Kate were sound asleep in the bunks above, and every so often in a lull of the wind, Adam could hear a little whistling snore from Mrs Perry. Only he was awake. Alone. Not scared. But worried. Worried about Lucy.

He knew he had to go to her. He had a feeling that she needed him. He took his flashlight from under his pillow, climbed out of bed as quietly as he could and crept into the passage. From a hook on the wall he took down a waterproof jacket which came to his knees, a sou'wester and a big black umbrella. Out on the verandah he found a pair of rubber boots which came up to his knees. He was ready for the storm.

As he stood on the steps the wind grabbed him and the rain spat at him. He stepped down off the verandah, the darkness swallowed him and suddenly Adam knew how Jonah must have felt. He could hear the river and he knew he must follow it in order to find Lucy, but he must not go too close because the banks would be slippery with the rain. He put his head down and set off.

It was a very long way in the dark. He kept as close to the river as he dared, so he knew he hadn't missed the willow tree. But it seemed much further than it ever did in the daytime. From time to time he flashed his light, but its weak little beam was lost in the heaving darkness. The boots, which were too large for him, slowed him down even more. His left foot slipped right out once, plunging him down in a squelching pool of mud, and he kept his balance only because of the umbrella which he was using as a walking stick.

Just as he was beginning to despair of ever finding the willow tree, he made out its swaying hump ahead of him and called to Lucy. But the wind gulped down his voice.

So he shone the light to let her know he was coming and he saw disaster.

The storm had split a big branch so that it dangled as useless as a broken arm. Lucy's shelter was destroyed. What about Lucy herself? And her eggs? Adam clambered through the wreckage of the tree, fearful of what he might find.

Lucy was sitting tight on her nest. At the approach of the flickering flashlight she pulled her head from under her wing and looked up at Adam. The General, squatting beside her, rose to his feet. Adam opened the umbrella and held it over them while he considered what he could do to help.

"I've got it, General," he exclaimed. "The sledge!"

He tramped off through the tangle of willow to look for it and dragged it back in triumph. Fumbling with cold wet fingers, he undid the ties on the wire netting and pulled the door into the ducks' enclosure. Carefully he manouvred it until he had it sloping down like a roof over Lucy, then he wedged it firmly against a fence post and the butt of the tree.

"There you are," he said proudly. "What more could you want?"

The General, who had been following Adam about, moved back in beside Lucy and the pair looked up at him gratefully.

"You're a good mother, Lucy. You deserve your eggs to hatch. And now you'll stay dry, even if the whole tree blows down," Adam declared. He tied up the enclosure again. "Safe as a house. Not that any sensible rats would come out in this weather, even water rats," he joked. "See you in the morning."

But it was no joke, rats or no rats, to start the long walk back alone. For a moment Adam was tempted to crawl in under the door with the ducks, but then he thought Mrs Perry would worry if she found that he was missing. So he hunched his shoulders against the wind and turned towards the house. The night wrapped itself round him like a cold wet flannel and Adam shivered inside his coat. He longed for a friendly presence and looked in vain for the moon or the winking eye of a star.

He thought he saw a light glimmering in the distance. Then he glimpsed a second light. Perhaps someone was coming out to look for him? Steve or Steve and Kate? There was a coo-ee and the light flashed off and on for a moment. Adam shouted back. The light was coming steadily closer.

Then he heard a voice calling, "Adam! Adam!" It was Mrs Perry. The sight of her big round face beaming down at him by the light of her lantern was a hundred times better than the moon. "I knew you'd be worried about Lucy in the storm," she said. She took the umbrella-walking stick from him, tucked his cold hand into her warm one and pushed up the umbrella so that it sheltered them both. Together they splashed back to the welcome light in the house and it did not seem far at all.

"Why don't you thaw out in a hot shower." Mrs Perry suggested, "while I make a warm drink." She rubbed his hair dry with a thick towel and opened up the door of the stove so that Adam could make toast over the coals.

"It was just as well I went," Adam told her, spearing a piece of bread on a fork. "A bough of the willow had broken and Lucy was sitting in the rain."

Back in bed, Adam thought of Lucy and The General safe and dry under their roof, and fell asleep.

# 6 ACCIDENT

The long summer days slipped by, sparkling like water in the river. Every morning and afternoon Adam faithfully carried out the goanna patrol. He labored at the foundations of the fence and lugged rocks up from the bank. Lucy sat contentedly on her eggs and Adam wondered every day when they would hatch and if he would see the ducklings before he had to leave. Meanwhile The General escorted Adam on his swimming practice and Adam knew he was getting better, stronger every day, and he could do more laps each time.

But the nights were not so good. Every

evening he put out the poisoned wheat. But he still had bad dreams about rats — stealthy, hungry, marauding rats, burrowing their way into Lucy's sanctuary, eating her eggs.

Then late one afternoon, as he was shutting in the fowls, he found the first reward for his careful routine.

"Mrs Perry, Mrs Perry," he yelled. "There's a dead rat! Come and see it! It's almost as big as Smutty." He burst into the kitchen to tell the good news.

Mrs Perry was dishing up and Kate was sitting at the table. "Charming," Kate said. "A delightful subject to discuss as we eat our stew."

But Mrs Perry was pleased. "Sounds like a king rat," she said.

"Oh, he is," Adam agreed.

"There'll be some more," Mrs Perry predicted.

"For sure," Adam said. "I'll bury them and keep a score."

"Charming," Kate repeated.

But Mrs Perry said, "Yes. Mark them up on the shed door. That's what my husband used to do when he had a blitz. I'll find you a piece of chalk after tea."

In the morning Adam found three more dead rats. He dug a hole down beyond the plum tree and had a ceremonial burying. He collected extra bread from Mrs Perry, gathered a pail full of snails from the iris bed for a celebration for Lucy and The General, and set off whistling.

He was halfway down the third paddock when a movement at the edge of the bush caught his eye. Did he see a whisk of rusty brown slipping behind the bracken? Or did he imagine it? Was it a fox? Or was it just sun on bark swaying in the wind? He watched and watched but there was no more to be seen.

He walked slowly on to the willow tree, wondering what he had seen, worrying again for Lucy and her eggs.

Lucy and The General enjoyed the snails, but Adam felt restless. He made two extra goanna patrols and he back-tracked to the place where he thought he had seen the fox. But there was not a trace of it to be found in the tussocky grass. He lugged more rocks from the river, so that the fence was solid stone inside and out along its base, and he tied the wire up with extra string when he left late in the afternoon.

Near the wheat bin in the shed he found another dead rat almost as big as the first. He marked it up on the tally board and went inside to Mrs Perry.

"We're up to five," he said. "But it's the foxes I'm worrying about now. I think I saw one this morning, down near the blackberries."

Mrs Perry nodded. "There used to be an old den there. Stan would dig it out once in a while. It's good cover for the rabbits, you see, and that brings the foxes."

Adam felt discouraged.

But Mrs Perry had a solution. "We'll have a blackberry picnic. If we all crash round there tomorrow that'll send them packing for a bit, long enough for Lucy's purposes anyway. And I could do with some extra hands to pick the berries this year. I'm right out of blackberry jam, and I guess you all like blackberry pie."

"Yum," said Kate. "But I'm afraid you'll have to count me out for picking. I've just got Daisy up to a very important stage. I don't want her to slacken off now."

"I have plans for tomorrow too," Steve said. "There's some caves further up the river I want to explore."

"Looks like you and me," Mrs Perry said to Adam. "We're a good team. We'll fix it."

Adam played a very bad game of Scrabble with Kate. "Really, you're hopeless," she said.

Then he had an even worse game of Mastermind with Steve. Steve said, "Well, I've done my duty by you. You could hardly call it fun. You might as well go to bed. You're not much good for anything else."

Mrs Perry said, "You'll hold my wool for me, won't you, while I wind it? You're much better than a chair, which is all I usually have these days."

So Adam held the wool, skein after skein of rusty brown wool, which Mrs Perry was knitting into a sweater for Stan, and as it wound from side to side he felt almost mesmerised.

He fell asleep straight away and had no dreams of rats. But the moon shining in the window woke him and the distant sound of a dog barking started him worrying about the foxes again. He could hardly wait for the morning.

After breakfast he took a mattock, a long-handled shovel and a bill-hook from the collection of tools in the shed, Mrs Perry brought sacks and pails and a basket, and together they trudged down to the blackberry patch. Adam heaved a few rocks into the thicket but nothing stirred. Mrs Perry, in big rubber boots and old overalls which had belonged to her husband, scouted about for fresh signs of the foxes.

"They could have been around," she said, "but the den's not in regular use, and they won't like the smell of us, so they won't stay long if they do come back."

The blackberries, just beginning to ripen, hung high in heavy clusters on the grabbing green brambles. Mrs Perry slashed at the thorny tangle and threw bags over it so that they could climb in where the fruit was thickest. She reached up and Adam picked low, and the billies were half filled. Adam hacked and trampled a new path deeper into the maze, his hands grew prickled and purple, and the billies were filled.

Mrs Perry produced sausage rolls, apple cake and lemonade and they sat down on a sack on the grass for their picnic.

"I don't think I've ever tasted better sausage rolls," Adam said. "You must be the best cook in Australia."

"I don't know about that." Mrs Perry laughed. "But I do know I've made a few miles of sausage rolls in my time. Stan was always very fond of sausage rolls."

She settled back against a tree and took out her knitting. "Haven't had a picnic like this for I don't know how long," she said. "It's a treat for me."

While she knitted, Adam went off and wielded the mattock around several little tunnels and holes in under the edges of the blackberry wall. And when he was out of sight of Mrs Perry he peed in some of them too. Not that she would have minded. He felt sure she would say that was just what Stan used to do.

At last she stood up. "If I'm going to make blackberry jam today, it's time I got started."

"What about coming down and seeing Lucy and The General?" Adam said. "It's not far and I'll help carry everything back."

"Might as well make a proper day of it," Mrs Perry agreed. "Dear old Lucy. She's a trier, that one. You're two of a kind," she said, pulling a blackberry leaf out of Adam's hair.

Adam was pleased at how Mrs Perry

50

admired the fence. "Do you think it will keep out the foxes?"

Mrs Perry was not inclined to guarantee it. "You never can tell with foxes," was all she would say.

Adam decided to fetch a few more stones to try to be on the safe side and Mrs Perry went with him down to the river.

Steve was just rounding the bend when a launch with a water-skier in tow came from the opposite direction, creating a strong wash. A second launch overtaking Steve zoomed by. The canoe, caught in the double wash, was swept against the rocky point and as Adam and Mrs Perry watched, Steve was flung out.

Adam ran, scrambling over stumps, jumping over tussocks. The canoe was drifting downstream fast. He waded out into the water. Deeper, deeper. Until he was bobbing. He struck out, kicking, thrusting, putting all his effort into every stroke. He grabbed the paddle as it winnowed by and with his other hand seized the bow of the canoe as it bore down on him.

It nearly pulled him under. But he kicked and kicked, and turned it slightly so that with the help of the current it was heading

inshore. His feet touched bottom. A snag
snatched at his leg. Weed wrapped around
him. But the canoe and the paddle were
safe. He dragged them up on to the bank.

Mrs Perry had run on up to the point.
Steve was sitting on the rocks, holding his
head. "Idiot boats," he was muttering.

"What a crack I collected from that rock."

Mrs Perry examined his head. A lump was already rising over his left eye. "Sit a bit longer," she suggested. "Then we'll just take it slowly home."

Adam ran along to the willow tree to his secret depot of emergency supplies. He took the three pieces of barley candy out of the can and brushed an ant off one. They were a bit sticky, but they were all right. He hurried back to Steve, peeling the paper off the candy as he went.

Steve was still holding his head. Adam pressed the barley candy into his hand. "I saved the canoe. And the paddle."

Steve only grunted.

With Mrs Perry on one side and Adam on the other he walked back to the house. Mrs Perry phoned the doctor. "He wants you overnight at the hospital for observation," she said when she hung up.

"I'm all right," Steve said.

"I think you are too, but I can't take risks with other people's children. Get into dry clothes, both of you, while I get the truck out."

Adam collected Steve's pajamas and toothbrush and put them in a plastic bag.

53

Then he went down to the garden fence and let out the longest whistle he could muster. Luckily Kate was in the home paddock. She came cantering over on Daisy.

"Steve's had an accident," Adam announced. "We're taking him in to the hospital. You'd better come." He helped her take off Daisy's saddle and bridle and turn her loose, then they ran back to the house together.

"I'll do the gates," Adam volunteered. Steve had ridden in the back of the truck when Mrs Perry had fetched them from the station at the beginning of the holidays and Adam had been envious. Now Steve was in the cab with Kate, and Adam was jumping off and on, opening, closing, feeling important.

They left Steve at the hospital in the care of a friendly nurse. "We'll come back and see you when you're settled," Mrs Perry said. They went down the main street. "Might as well do some shopping while we're here," Mrs Perry said. They went to the supermarket and bought sugar, flour, tea, vinegar and spices, and a bag of peppermints for Steve.

Then they went to the newsagent for a

magazine for Steve. "One with plenty of pictures," Mrs Perry suggested. "He mightn't feel much like reading. In fact he might not even be allowed." Adam felt quite sorry for Steve. It would be awful not to be allowed to read. For once he hoped Mrs Perry might be wrong. In the street they met a friend of Mrs Perry, who invited them to her place for tea. Then they went back to the hospital where Steve was sitting up in bed watching TV.

It was dark when they left to drive back to the farm. Adam was not sorry to be in the cab again now as the black bush bulged with strange shapes in the headlights of the truck.

Just before they reached the turn-off to the farm, he saw a dark patch on the road. "What's that, Mrs Perry?"

Mrs Perry slowed down and in the lights they could see a body. A long body with four legs and a big tail.

"It's a fox," Mrs Perry said with satisfaction. "A dog fox by the look of it. Good news for the chooks."

And for Lucy and The General, Adam thought. But he didn't say anything in front of Kate. She would only make fun of him and his ducks.

Then Mrs Perry said, "We'd better put the chooks in, all the same. There'll be a vixen about somewhere."

Adam felt anxious again. It didn't seem to matter what happened. Mrs Perry was right. You couldn't guarantee that Lucy and her eggs would be safe.

Together they took the lanterns and went down into the orchard. The fowls were in the apple trees. "Wouldn't they be safer here up in the branches, if a fox comes?" Adam asked Mrs Perry in a whisper.

"No," Mrs Perry said. "You see, they panic if they're disturbed, and the fox has no problem." She started talking to the hens before she shone the light on them and they began stirring sleepily, clucking and muttering under their wings. Gently Mrs Perry shooed them down out of the trees and drove them back into the yard.

A white one turned away in a fluster just before it reached the gate, and Adam chased it round the mandarin tree and almost up to the back door before he caught it. At last they dropped the latch down and headed towards the house.

"What about the picnic things and the

blackberries?'' Adam asked.

"They can wait till tomorrow," Mrs Perry said.

"I'll just do the poison baits then."

"Don't worry about them tonight," Mrs Perry said.

But Adam was determined. The fox was a bonus. But he'd had to miss two goanna patrols because of Steve's accident and the rats were not going to miss out on their treatment for the same reason. He went off to the shed with the lantern.

"Two more," he reported when he came into the kitchen.

"How many does that make it?" Mrs Perry asked.

"Fourteen."

"And there'll be more you haven't found." Mrs Perry's certainty was like a reward.

# 7 THE TROPHY

Adam's first job in the morning was to fetch the blackberries, so that Mrs Perry could get the jam made before she had to go in to the hospital to collect Steve.

The pails were sitting on the grass under the tree, just as they had left them, except that a slug had crawled up into one, leaving its silvery trail over the blackened metal and through the hills and dales of berries. Adam tossed out the silvered ones and looked for the slug. Its track did not go down the other side of the billy, so it must still be in there somewhere, sleeping off its supper. He'd have to remember to tell Mrs Perry to find it, otherwise it'd be blackberry and slug jam, and no one would ever know.

He inspected his diggings and slashings. There were no tracks or droppings to be seen. He peed into one of the tunnels for luck, then gathered up the tools, the sacks, the picnic basket and the pails and trudged back to the house.

He brought in the big jam pan from its hook on the back verandah and told Mrs Perry about the slug. Then he went off to move the canoe to a safer place up the bank.

Funny, he thought, as he heaved and lifted it up the steep slope. Funny that no one even noticed that I swam out, actually swam out and rescued this canoe. If it hadn't been for me, swimming out into the river, it would probably be bobbing along in the Pacific Ocean by now.

He paused on top of the bank, judging the distance back to the shed. It would be a tough one-man transport job, he decided, and wondered how Stan used to manage. Easier to leave it here for the time being. But he'd take the paddle back. As he walked with the paddle light on his shoulder, he thought about the fox. It would be interesting to have a closer look at it.

He propped the paddle up in a corner of the shed and as he did so, he noticed a big old knife among the tools on the wall. He took it down carefully. It was heavy. He tried it out on a chunk of rope. Nothing wrong with that. He rather fancied the idea of that fox's tail as a good-luck trophy. The knife was just what he needed.

The road was long and empty, stretching out like a strip of unused sandpaper. On either side black cockatoos flapping through the tall trees followed a flight pattern that would have baffled any air traffic controller. And a hidden orchestra of cicadas netted the bush with shrill strands of sound. Adam was always on the lookout for a black cicada, but today the fox was his goal and he did not turn aside once.

At last in the distance he saw a blot. It partly dissolved as nine crows rose, protesting at his approach. They perched overhead in the trees, asserting raucously that first come was first served.

Adam looked at the meal he had interrupted. The sun was hot on it and oily green blowflies already swarmed and buzzed above it. "You can have it and welcome," he told the crows. For a moment he thought they might have his breakfast as well. But he turned his back on the pointed head with its sharp nose and prick ears, and hacked at the base of the tail with determination. After all it would have taken more than a squashed fox to make Stan throw up.

It was a good knife. Four chops and the tail lay severed. Adam fished in his pocket for a piece of string, picked up a stick and tied the brush to it.

"Go to it," he told the crows, though they needed no urging. He had only put five meters between himself and the fox when they were already returning to their feast.

Brush dangling triumphantly over his shoulder, he returned home. There was a heavy sweet smell of jam as he stopped outside the kitchen window. Mrs Perry was washing up. He waved the fox brush at her. She waved the dishmop back.

"I'm going to nail it up on the willow tree for Lucy and The General," Adam announced.

"Just the thing," Mrs Perry said. "But

wait a tick. I must get a photo of this for Stan.''

Adam felt ten feet tall as he posed.

"How's the jam going?'' he remembered to enquire, as Mrs Perry put the camera away.

"First batch is finished and in the jars. And the second batch is on the way,'' she reported. "As soon as it's done, we'd better make tracks for the hospital.''

"It smells pretty good. Better than the fox.''

"I reckon.'' Mrs Perry laughed. Adam loved her laugh. It was rich and chuckling and bubbling. Just like the sound of the blackberry jam gurgling deep in the belly of the pan on the stove.

"You'd better try some before you go off again,'' she said. "Wash your hands well and you can get me some more jars from the cupboard in the laundry, while I cut the bread.''

It was good jam. Adam had three slices with it thick and lumpy, sweet and shiny. Then he said, "I'd better go. That goanna'll be getting ideas again if I'm not around.'' He went off with the fourth slice in one hand and the stick with the fox brush in the other.

Kate was in the third paddock with Daisy.
Adam kept well to the river side. Though
Kate had the horse well in hand now, if
Daisy got ideas in her head Kate would
blame it on him. Anyway he didn't want her
to see his trophy in case she tried to bag it.

Kate noticed Adam and put Daisy into a
gallop. He watched, feeling a little envious
still, when suddenly Daisy stopped short
and reared. Kate flew off and lay on the
grass while Daisy whinnied, then charged
away at a wild gait.

Adam sprinted, fox tail flying out
behind. Kate was sitting up, pulling faces,
when he reached her.

63

"Rotten fox," she burst out. "Just when I was really getting Daisy into her stride."

"Come off it," Adam said. "You can't blame me for that."

"You?" said Kate. "I'm not blaming you. I tell you, it was a fox in the bracken there that made her shy."

"Another fox?" Adam started to run towards the bracken, shouting and whirling the brush over his head.

Daisy, who had been coming round in smaller, slower circles, took off again in new fright.

"Are you mad?" Kate yelled. "Come and help me up. And calm down or we'll never catch that horse."

Adam walked back to her. "Are you all right?"

"Now you ask!" Kate said. "Much you care if I've broken my arm."

"I'm sorry if you've hurt yourself, but you don't sound any different." He helped her to her feet. "Don't worry about Daisy. I'll walk back to the house with you in case you faint. Then I'll come back and take off her saddle and rub her down. She'll let me do it by then."

"Where did you get that brush?" Kate

64

wanted to know as they made their way back.

"From the fox that was run over last night."

"I wouldn't mind having it as a souvenir," Kate said.

"Sorry," said Adam. "I've promised it to someone else."

Mrs Perry looked at Kate's white face and limp arm. "They say troubles always come in threes. Never mind, we'll get them to have a look at you at the hospital when we collect Steve. Just lie down there on the sofa while I finish bottling this jam and then we'll be off."

"I'll see to Daisy," Adam said. "Give me a hoot when you're ready." He went off down the paddock armed with sugar, apples and Daisy's brush. He whistled and she came to him as if she had never seen a fox in her life.

"What about it, old girl?" he said, as she took an apple from him. He hitched her to the gatepost and struggled with the straps. At last she was unsaddled, and he climbed on to the gate to reach her better while he brushed her down. She stood patient and unmoving until he had finished.

Adam looked towards the shed and wondered if there was time for a quick goanna patrol before they left, but he had hardly gone ten paces when he heard the truck horn. He picked up the saddle and bridle and hurried back. "Do I have to go? There's things I really ought to be doing here."

"I'm sure there are," Mrs Perry said. "But I would like a hand with the gates."

"Of course," Adam said and hopped in.

There was a delay at the hospital before Kate's arm could be X-rayed and treated, so Mrs Perry and Adam went down the street again. It seemed to Adam that everyone knew Mrs Perry and stopped to talk with her. But while she was chatting and laughing, he was worrying. If only he'd had a chance to do one goanna patrol. If only he'd had a chance to follow that fox.

At last Steve and Kate were discharged from the hospital. Steve had been given a clean bill of health, but the doctor told Mrs Perry he was to take things quietly for a few days. "No canoeing." Kate's injury was only a sprained wrist, but she was debarred from riding until it was better.

Mrs Perry was pleased. "All's well that

ends well. I'm glad I don't have to tell your parents any bad news.''

Kate and Steve were not so happy. ''What am I going to do if I can't canoe? We might as well go home,'' Steve said. Kate chimed in, ''No riding for days! And I've spent the whole of the holidays getting Daisy up to the stage where I can do some real riding. Now it's all wasted. There's nothing else I want to do. I agree. Why don't we go home? After all, we'd be going soon anyway.''

Adam was embarrassed for Mrs Perry's sake and worried on account of Lucy and The General. For him every remaining day was precious. He did want to be around when the eggs hatched. He said stoutly, ''There's no reason to talk about going home. This is as good as home. Better. Mrs Perry's the best cook in Australia and there's loads to do. There's heaps of things I planned for today I haven't had time for.''

''Such as?'' Kate enquired.

Adam didn't answer.

''Duck watching, I suppose, or perhaps fox hunting?''

Adam was glad to escape by climbing into the back of the truck again. He wasn't so happy himself either. Mrs Perry's saying that troubles always come in threes niggled at the back of his mind and he was in a ferment of impatience to get home to Lucy and The General. It was not yet quite dark and if he hurried he would be able to make a quick check on them.

"I'll do the chooks when I get back," Adam told Mrs Perry as he hopped off the truck. She nodded.

"Back from where?" Kate asked.

But Adam was already on his way to the willow tree.

# 8 NIGHT RAIDER

There was still some light in the western sky and the colors of the river, the paddocks and the bordering bush were distinct though muted. But the trees were turning dark and the hills were hunching themselves into heavy night shapes. In the east the moon, full at last, was rising. It gleamed like a big etched pearlshell disc Adam had seen at the museum in a case with spears and masks and feather shoes worn by men who made magic.

A heron flapped its slow way up river, and down on the flat a plover cried. Adam shivered a little. Not that it was cold. But there was a feeling in the air. A feeling that something would happen this night. Whether it was something good or something bad he didn't know. He hoped it was not going to be the third trouble of Mrs Perry's proverb.

He was almost to the third paddock when he saw it. The movement caught his eye first. Then the color. Sandy-reddish-clayish. Then the shape. A fox. The fox. Slipping out of the bracken. Heading across the corner. Through the fence. Along the blackberries. Towards the fowl yard. And the chickens were still out.

Adam turned and ran. Fast, faster. Faster than he'd ever run in all his life.

He flung the kitchen door open and

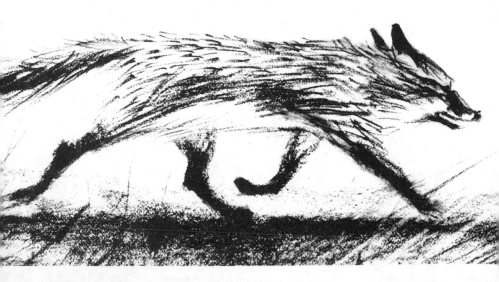

panted the urgent message. "I saw it! It's coming this way!"

Mrs Perry was sitting in her chair by the stove, knitting. In one moment she'd laid down her knitting and stood up. Without a word she went out of the room, along the passage.

"What's this mysterious 'it'?" Steve laughed.

"Is 'it' a ghost?" Kate wanted to know. "I hope so. The place needs a bit of livening up."

Mrs Perry's sudden reappearance carrying a shotgun silenced them.

Then Steve got up. "I didn't know you had that," he said.

"No?" Mrs Perry said, picking up the flashlight which was kept in the cupboard by the door, and handing it to Adam.

"I'll come with you," Steve said.

"No," said Mrs Perry. "One's enough. Adam knows all about it."

They went out quickly and quietly into the darkening garden. After the lighted room it was hard to see, but in a moment Adam's eyes were accustomed again to the dark. He scanned the paddock for a moving form. There was nothing to be seen.

Then suddenly down by the lemon tree there was a red glint. Adam touched Mrs Perry's arm. She nodded. She'd seen it. "Cheeky brute!" she muttered, but so softly that Adam could only just hear.

In the next instant the report of the gun filled his ears and made him jump sideways right into the rhubarb bed.

"Dropped it, I think," Mrs Perry said. "Let's have a look."

They moved silently towards the lemon tree. "Light now," she said.

"Ah!" they both exclaimed as the roving beam brought the limp body of a well-grown fox into view.

The quietness was shattered again by shouts and the pounding of feet as Kate and Steve raced through the garden in search of them.

"Whatever's happened?" Kate called.

"Everything all right?" Steve asked.

They came up to Mrs Perry and Adam staring at the fox.

"I bags the brush," Kate said. "After all, I deserve it, seeing this is probably the fox which made Daisy shy so that I sprained my wrist."

"Sorry," said Mrs Perry. "It's already

promised." She grinned at Adam. "We'll just put a sack over this now till morning."

"And then," Adam continued, "we'll take a photo for Stan. You're a dead shot," he said proudly to Mrs Perry.

Back on the verandah she was about to unload the other barrel when Steve said, "Can I have a turn with it tomorrow?"

"Have a turn?" said Mrs Perry. "And what would you have a turn at?"

"Aw, crows, or something like that." Steve hadn't really thought.

"Firearms are only used for vermin on this property, by people who know how to handle them."

"I've done a bit of target practice at school," Steve said.

"We'll see how good you are then," Mrs Perry said, reloading. She led the way to the implement shed. In the moonlight they saw a rat running towards the haystack. Mrs Perry took aim. The rat stopped in its tracks, never to run again.

"It's a pretty small target," Steve said.

"Yes," said Mrs Perry, firing at a second rat which had scuttled out from the cover of a bale, to which it would not return.

"But if *you* can do it . . ." he said.

Mrs Perry did not wait for him to finish before she slipped in two more cartridges and handed the gun to him.

They waited.

"Boring," said Kate. "I'm going back."

Nobody answered. She went.

They waited. Steve said, "You've scared them."

"I doubt it," Mrs Perry said. "Rats don't scare easily."

As if to prove her right, as well as a good shot, another rat obligingly came out of the stack. Steve aimed at it but it had disappeared while his finger was squeezing the trigger. He fired at an empty space. "Better luck next time," he muttered. "Takes a bit to get your eye in."

They waited.

Another rat, or the same one, emerged from a different place. Steve was quicker this time, but missed. "Narrow escape," he said. "He was a lucky devil."

Mrs Perry didn't say anything.

Adam said, "I'll go and shut the chooks in and put out the poison."

"Let me have one more go," Steve said.

"Third time lucky," Adam chanted.

Steve pretended not to hear.

"No," said Mrs Perry. "It's been a long day. I don't want you late to bed, after what the doctor said, and we haven't even eaten yet."

Adam wasn't really listening. He was looking up at the moon. It had changed from a pearlshell full of magic and spells to something much more homely. Now all orange and gold, it reminded him of something else that Mrs Perry made better than anyone he knew. "Pancake," he said, "with orange marmalade."

"What a good idea," said Mrs Perry. "I'll make some for supper."

"I'll be quick with the chooks then," Adam said.

"Do you want me to help?" Steve asked.

Adam shook his head. "They know me. You might scare them. I'll be quicker by myself."

Supper was ready when he came in and Adam celebrated the death of the second fox by eating three man-in-the-moon marmalade pancakes.

# 9 LEMON MERINGUE

Next morning Adam was itching to be off to see Lucy and The General. But first there was breakfast and then chickens' breakfast before the ceremonial inspection and photo of the fox carcass.

At breakfast Mrs Perry proposed another picnic. "It's a good day today. We'd better make the most of it. This time next week you'll be back at school. And it's not much fun going for a picnic by myself."

Kate said, "Might as well," almost graciously for her. Then she spoiled it by adding, "Seeing there's nothing else to do. But I won't be able to pick blackberries, because of my wrist."

77

"I wasn't thinking of blackberries," Mrs Perry said. "You've all been so busy, there are lots of places you haven't explored yet."

"Such as?" said Kate.

"You'll see," was all that Mrs Perry would say. She organised Kate and Steve to do the washing up while she put the lunch together and Adam fed the fowls. Then they all went out with the camera to look at the fox. Adam carried the knife.

The fox stretched out under the lemon tree looked beautiful with the morning sun glinting on its thick rusty pelt. Adam felt almost sad about it lying so still and stiff with the ants tracking up to its eyes.

But Mrs Perry had no pity for it. "It's a vixen all right, and good riddance." She brushed the belly with the toe of her shoe. "And she's not feeding cubs, so that's a few troubles the less, too."

Adam took a photo of her beside it before he cut off the brush. Then he said, "Shall we bury it somewhere?"

"Not worth wasting the time and effort," Mrs Perry said. "Drag it up into the bush and let the crows fix it. That's what Stan used to do."

Adam fetched a piece of rope from the

shed and tied it round one of the fox's front paws. "I'll give you a hand," Steve said. As they took it in turns dragging the carcass up the hill he said, "It'd be good to have the brush to show the fellas at school when I tell them how we shot a fox in the holidays. I wonder who Mrs Perry's promised it to."

"Stan, maybe," Adam said, and dropped the subject.

Back in the home paddock Kate was waiting with Daisy. "Just give me a hand saddling her up, will you?" she said to Adam. "I don't want her to get too collar proud before I ride her again."

With only orders from Kate, Adam managed to get Daisy saddled.

"That'll have to do," Kate said. "Now I think you'd better ride her to keep her quiet."

Adam could hardly believe his ears.

"You'd better put on my hard hat."

It fitted almost perfectly.

"I'm off," Adam announced.

"Oh no you're not," Kate said. "I'm leading."

"But I'm in a hurry," Adam protested.

"You'll get there faster this way," Kate said, "than if you took off on your own."

So they went down the home paddock at a walking pace. At first, Adam, impatient to get to Lucy and The General, fretted at the slowness. But as he fell in with the rhythm of Daisy's gait and began to look around him, he started enjoying his new vantage point.

Then as they breasted the rise at last and looked down past the willow tree to the backwater, Adam was the first to be able to see. Lucy and The General were both out swimming, and between them was a string of ducklings — six, seven, eight, nine ducklings, little lemon meringue ducklings, bobbing along beside their parents.

Adam had no words for the happiness he felt. He beamed at the duck family and turned to Mrs Perry who had just seen them. She took a deep breath and then summed it up very satisfactorily. "This'll be something to tell Stan!" Her shiny red cheeks bulged like apples as she smiled up at

him. She put up her left hand to him. "Congratulations!" Adam slid down and hugged her.

Kate said, "You should have got off the other side. But never mind. You'll learn. Are those your ducks?"

Adam nodded.

"The babies are cute, but I hope they don't grow up looking like their father. What a schnozzle he's got!"

"He looks a fierce brute," Steve commented.

"He is too, when he needs to be," Adam agreed. "He's not called The General for nothing. But he's all right when he gets to know you."

"What about the white one? She looks rather nice," Kate said.

"Lucy? Oh, she is," Adam said warmly. "She's been so patient all the holidays, sitting on the eggs. But Mrs Perry, there were thirteen eggs and there are only nine ducklings. Nine's a good number, better than thirteen, but what happened to the rest? Do you think the rats got them?" he asked, suddenly anxious.

"Probably didn't hatch," Mrs Perry said in her matter-of-fact way. "Usually a few don't. But why don't we go and look? Lucy won't mind strangers near her nest now."

Kate and Steve followed them into the green willow tent.

"Say, this is cool," said Kate, gazing up at the thick green ceiling.

But Steve's attention was taken by the wire netting enclosure and the shelter. "Did you build that, man?" he asked. "It's real neat."

Proudly Adam turned to show off Lucy's nest, lined with the down from her own breast. There were still four eggs in it. Mrs Perry touched them lightly. "Cold," she said. "They won't hatch now. We'd better get rid of them. They'll only bring the rats around."

Rats. Still rats to worry about.

Then Steve spoke up. "I can see now why you seemed to have rats on the brain, young Adam. And it would be rotten if they got to the ducklings after all this. I really would like to try to shoot some, if you'll let me, Mrs Perry. I have some pocket money and if we're going in to town again, I could buy some ammo and put in some proper practice in the daytime. Then I'll have more chance of knocking them off."

Mrs Perry smiled at him. "Glad to have another recruit for the rat campaign, aren't we, Adam? But you've no need to spend your pocket money. I've got plenty of cartridges and I'm happy for them to be used sensibly and for the right reason. Now what about nicking back and getting the camera, so we can take a photo of the new family for Stan?" she said to Adam.

"You might as well ride Daisy," Kate said. "But mind you only walk her. And while you're at the house will you get my painting gear out of my case? I haven't used it yet these holidays and this'd be super to paint. If you like it, and if it's good enough of course," Kate added almost shyly, "you might like to have it as a souvenir of our visit," she suggested to Mrs Perry.

"Sounds a lovely idea to me," Mrs Perry said warmly.

Kate wandered away happily to choose the angle for her painting and Adam went off alone on Daisy.

"Don't hurry," Mrs Perry called after him "We have all day."

Daisy stepped it out quite willingly to the house. Adam quickly found the camera and Kate's painting gear. Then with a sudden secret hope he went to the shed and fetched the paddle. He balanced it against the fence and picked it up again after he had mounted. Daisy was not in the least bothered at having it across her and she didn't seem to mind a bit either that Adam sang all the way back, a song he made up as he went, about a big dappled horse, two brave ducks, two dead foxes and a horde of rats.

Steve was watching for them. "What've you brought the paddle for? You know I'm not allowed in the canoe."

"I thought maybe I could paddle it back to the house," Adam said. "It'd be easier than carrying it."

"You? But you can't swim."

"Who said I can't? Who do you think swam out in the river and rescued the canoe and the paddle when you were thrown out?" Adam decided not to waste time arguing. He kicked off his thongs, peeled off his T-shirt and jumped in with the ducks. "Don't let me disturb you, Lucy. I won't bother your babies," he called as he set off on his first lap. The General swam after him and the pair of them swam up and down, up and down.

"You touching the bottom?" Steve called.

Adam spluttered indignantly, "I am not," and went on swimming up and down, up and down, The General at his side.

"OK. I believe you," Steve called. "You've proved your point."

But Adam had a point to prove to himself as well. Today he would swim twenty lengths — one for each of the ducklings and one each for Lucy and The General, one for Daisy, one for Kate, one for Steve, one for Mrs Perry, one for Stan and four for the canoe. That would be the most he'd ever swum. Ducklings...Lucy...The General ...Daisy...Kate...Steve...Mrs Perry... Stan...canoe...in out, in out...

Slowly he came out at last up the bank. Mrs Perry was sitting with Lucy, who had already gathered up her young swimmers for a while. "What about it?" he wanted to know. "Can I paddle the canoe back to the house?"

"I don't see why not," she said, "provided you wear the life jacket."

"Dummy me," Adam said. "I forgot to bring it. Daisy and I'll go back and get it."

"After lunch," Mrs Perry said. "We

have all day." She began unpacking the baskets.

It was the best picnic Adam had ever known. But as he peeled his hard-boiled egg he had a sudden thought which almost spoiled it. "What about the goanna?" he said to Mrs Perry.

"I don't think you need worry too much about him for a while. He's probably found the fox by now and is having the feed of his life. Anyway he's just as likely to eat rats as ducklings." Mrs Perry threw some bread to the ducks.

Adam was reassured, but he wasn't taking any chances. "I'll just do a quick patrol," he said.

"I'll come with you," Steve offered.

Adam gave him a can and a stick and they went off together, banging and laughing.

"Any self-respecting goanna will soon clear out with that racket," Mrs Perry told him when they came back.

Adam grinned and said, "Now I'll just zap back and pick up that life jacket."

"If Daisy can carry you after all that lunch you've eaten," Kate said. But she was only joking.

Adam came back on foot, wearing the

life jacket. "Thought I'd save you the trouble of leading Daisy again," he said to Kate.

"Thanks," she said. "And it would be great if you wouldn't mind exercising her tomorrow."

"Sure," Adam replied. "Coming?" he said to Steve.

They walked down the bank together. Steve helped lift the canoe to the water's edge and held it while Adam stepped in. One push and he was off, riding the river at last, the rippling running river whose music and movement had been the background to all his days and nights on the farm. In and out with the paddle, in and out, in and out, then almost as soon as he had begun it seemed, it was time to be turning in to the bank again. Adam sighed as he pulled in to the landing place.

Steve had followed him down and gave a hand to lift the canoe out. "That was better than portaging," he said. "You managed well. I'll tell you a few techniques tomorrow. Meantime, how would it be if we rig up a couple of rat traps down near the ducks? I reckon I'd be nearly as sorry as you if anything happened to those little fellas."

They carried the canoe up to the shed. "I know where there's wire and a couple of boxes," Adam said.

"Good," Steve said. "And we'll need a couple of springs or perhaps we could rig up some levers and weights."

Back at the willow tree they worked side by side for the rest of the afternoon. When it was time to go home, Adam shut in the ducks. Then he looked with satisfaction at the contraptions he and Steve had built to beat any rats that might dare to fancy a duck dinner.

"Nearly as good as Stan might have made, don't you think?" he ventured to say to Mrs Perry.

"No doubt about it," she replied. "Even Stan couldn't have done better."